For Ruby

Special thanks to Val Wilding

First published in 2012
by Faber and Faber Ltd
Bloomsbury House
74–77 Great Russell Street
London WC1B 3DA

Printed in England by CPI Group (UK) Ltd, Croydon, CR0 4YY

Designed and typeset by Mandy Norman
Series created by Working Partners Limited, London W6 0QT

A CIP record for this book
is available from the British Library

978–0–571–25986–1

FSC
www.fsc.org
MIX
Paper from
responsible sources
FSC® C101712

2 4 6 8 10 9 7 5 3 1

Magic Toyshop

Treasure Island Trouble

By Jessie Little

Illustrated by Penny Dann

ff

faber and faber

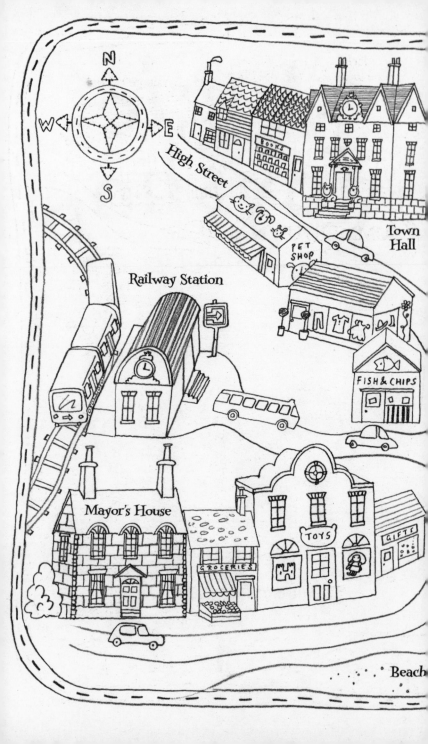

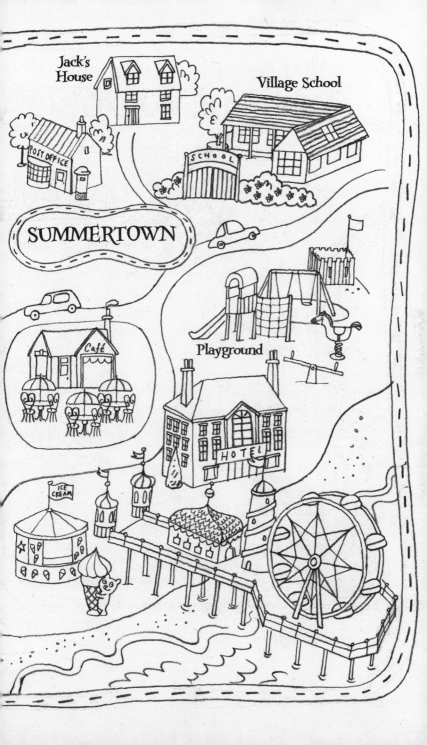

WHO LIVES IN SUMMERTOWN?
MEET THE HOOZLES!

This is
Willow and Toby

Here are Freddie
and Wobbly

Aunt Suzy
owns the toyshop!

The Hoozle Council – Grouchy, Wizard and Lovely

Spike the pufferfish is new!

Nasty Croc is the only mean Hoozle

Chapter One

Willow hugged her Hoozle bear, Toby, as she followed Auntie Suzy and her brother, Freddie, on to Summertown Pier. 'I wonder where we're going,' she whispered to him. 'I'm so excited!'

There were lots of people on the

pier, so Toby didn't move and he
didn't speak.

As they walked, Willow looked
through the cracks between the
wooden slats of the pier to see the sea
glinting below.

'Wobbly's
excited, too!'
cried Freddie,
waving his
lion Hoozle.
'He wants to
know what's
happening.'

Auntie Suzy turned. The wind whipped her yellow curls around her face, making her laugh. 'I told you; it's a surprise,' she said. 'You've been so helpful in my toy shop this summer that I want to give you a reward.'

'But why did you make us wear wellies?' asked Willow, as they passed the Pier End Cafe. 'It's not raining.'

Freddie ran to the railing. 'Look at that big boat!'

Willow went to see. The boat's name was painted on the side in curly letters. 'It's called *Sharkfin*,' she told Freddie. Then she noticed a sign fixed to the railings. It said:

Boat trip today!
✫ **Sail on *Sharkfin* to Summertown Cove**
✫ **Guided tour of the Great Caves**
✫ **Please wear wellington boots and bring a torch**

Willow spun round. 'Auntie Suzy, is that why you told us to wear wellies?'

'Yes, it is,' she replied with a big
smile.

Freddie jumped up and down.
'We're going on a boat! We're going
on a boat!' He ran to join the queue
of people waiting to climb aboard.

They were all putting on yellow lifejackets. Freddie, Willow and Auntie Suzy had to put one on, too.

'I have something for Toby and Wobbly,' said Auntie Suzy. She burrowed in her huge orange handbag and took out two tiny, bright yellow lifejackets. 'Everyone who goes to sea should wear one,' she said.

'Especially Hoozles!' Willow cried in delight. As she put Toby's on she could see he was thrilled with his new jacket. 'You look great,' she whispered.

'Thanks,' he said in his quietest growly voice.

When it was Willow's turn to board the boat, she climbed down the steps to a platform, then crossed the gangplank. A man held out his hand to help her and said, 'Welcome aboard *Sharkfin*, young lady, and welcome to your Hoozle, too.'

Once she was safely across the gangplank, Willow turned to say thank you and giggled. The man had a Hoozle parrot stuck on his shoulder with a strip of Velcro tape.

'I'm Captain Price,' said the man, 'and when I bought *Sharkfin* your Auntie Suzy gave me my very own Hoozle to wish me good luck. He's called Mr Squawk.'

'Hello, Mr Squawk.' Willow held Toby's paw and made him wave. She wasn't too surprised when the parrot slowly winked, then wiggled just the very tip of his bright blue wing. After all, she knew the Hoozle secret – that they were all alive!

Freddie jumped aboard by himself. When Captain Price saw Wobbly he said, 'Goodness! Two Hoozle passengers today.' He hugged Auntie Suzy. 'Welcome aboard, all of you!'

Auntie Suzy led the way to the front of the boat where a boy about Willow's age was sitting on the deck tying a thick rope into a big knot. He wore a dark-blue- and white-striped T-shirt and had a red pirate sash tied round his waist. 'Hi, Suzy,' he said. Then he turned to Willow and Freddie. 'I'm Ben. The captain is my uncle, and I help him with the boat trips.'

Willow noticed a blue and yellow
toy dangling from Ben's belt. 'That's a
Hoozle!' she said. 'What's his name?'

'Spike,' said Ben. 'He's a puffer fish
Hoozle.' He looked at Toby. 'Nice
bear.'

'Thanks,' said Willow.

'And your lion's really cool,' Ben said to Freddie.

'I know,' said Freddie. Then he asked, 'Why is Spike called a puffer fish?

'Because when puffer fish are in danger,' said Ben, 'they can puff themselves up really big and scare away their enemies.'

Freddie laughed. 'I could do that.' He blew out his cheeks and showed Auntie Suzy how big and fearsome he was.

Just then, Captain Price called, 'All aboard and ready to go, young Ben. Cast off!'

Ben scrambled over some seats to where a rope tied *Sharkfin* to the pier. 'Ready Captain!' he yelled.

Captain Price hauled the gangplank on board, and Ben untied the rope and pulled it on to the deck.

Once the engine was running, he untied the other rope and they were away.

'We're off, Toby,' Willow whispered to her Hoozle. Nobody heard her, because of the engine noise.

Toby squeezed her thumb. 'I've never been to sea before,' he growled softly.

'Don't worry,' she replied. 'You'll be safe.'

Ben came over and began sorting out a pile of ropes.

'Can I help?' Willow asked.

'Better not,' said Ben. 'I've sailed a lot, so I know what I'm doing.'

'I bet I could learn to do anything you can do,' said Willow. 'You'd only need to show me once.'

'OK,' said Ben. 'I'll teach you to tie some sailors' knots.'

He showed her how to tie an anchor bend knot. 'This is for fixing a rope to an anchor,' he explained.

When Willow had had a few goes, Ben said, 'That's not bad.'

She grinned. 'I think I'm pretty good. Let's have a knot-tying race.'

Ben shrugged and said, 'Okay. Ready, steady . . . go!'

Willow's fingers flew! Her knot was  done and pulled tight, a split second before Ben finished. 'Wow!' he said. 'You're right. You *are* pretty good. But I still know more knots than you.'

Willow was about to say she could easily learn any knot Ben knew, when Captain Price called the passengers to gather round.

'Go and listen,' said Ben. 'I've heard the story before.'

'What story?' asked Willow.

Ben leaned forward. 'The story,' he hissed, 'of the ghost of Six-Fingered Jim!'

Willow shivered with excitement. 'Ooooh!'

Chapter Two

Willow wedged herself and Toby
between Freddie and Auntie Suzy.

'Are you ready for the tale of the
ghost of Six-Fingered Jim?' asked
Captain Price.

'Yes!' the passengers yelled.

The Captain began. 'Six-Fingered

Jim was a wicked pirate! In days gone by, he hid from the King's navy in Summertown Cove.'

Willow held tight to Toby. A real pirate? In Summertown Cove?

Captain Price told how Six-Fingered Jim captured a great ship, full of gold coins and jewels and all sorts of treasures. 'He sailed away in his pirate ship, *Peg Leg's Revenge*, and the King's sailors hunted him for months. They chased him across the seven seas. Then one day, Six-Fingered Jim anchored the *Peg Leg's*

Revenge . . .' The captain looked around, shading his eyes, '. . . on this very spot.'

Willow felt Toby grip her thumb. Freddie clung to Wobbly.

The captain continued, 'It was Six-Fingered Jim's birthday, and he threw a party. Those pirates ate, and they drank, and they danced the sailor's hornpipe, and they sang sea songs until they were so tired that they fell asleep on deck.'

'Then what happened?' asked a wide-eyed boy.

'The King's sailors found them,' said Captain Price. 'There was a terrible fight, with guns and cannon and cutlasses! A few pirates escaped, and some were locked up in prison. But Six-Fingered Jim was never seen again. Well, not in the flesh . . .'

A man asked, 'What do you mean, not in the flesh?'

'The treasure was never found,' said Captain Price. 'They say that Six-Fingered Jim hid it in a cavern deep in the caves of Summertown Cove – a cavern that's shaped like the mouth of a tiger!'

'Treasure,' Willow whispered to Toby. 'I'd like to find that!'

Captain Price spoke again. 'Ay, the treasure might be there, but so is something else.'

'What?' everyone cried.

Captain Price leaned
forward and said in a low
voice, 'The ghost of Six-
Fingered Jim!'

Willow felt Toby shiver.
She stroked his soft blue
head.

'His ghost haunts that
cavern,' said the captain,
'and it guards the treasure.'
He held up a warning

hand. 'Beware. They say
that anyone who seeks the
treasure just . . . *disappears*!
Never, ever to be seen again.
It's the curse of Six-Fingered
Jim!'

Willow felt uneasy. Toby
leaned against her shoulder
and whispered, 'It's only
a story, Willow. Don't be
frightened. I'm here.'

She hugged him, and noticed that she wasn't the only one who found the story of Six-Fingered Jim creepy. Several of the children looked a bit scared.

Captain Price laughed. 'Never fear. We're only going to explore the beautiful caves you can see in the cliff ahead, so you're in no danger.'

Willow was relieved that none of the caves looked anything like the mouth of a tiger. She went to see if Ben knew any more about the pirate treasure and found him sitting behind a chest of tools. As she drew near, she heard him talking to someone.

'Why can't we have a swim?' a small voice pleaded. 'I promise I'll stay out of sight.'

Ben's voice said, 'If we swim now, I could lose you. Be patient and wait till later.'

'I'm always patient,' said the voice. 'Good old patient Spike, that's me.'

Spike? Willow's heart leapt. She peeked over the chest.

It *was* Spike! Ben was talking to his Hoozle! So he knew the secret, too.

Ben looked up. 'Oh, I wasn't . . . I didn't . . . I mean, I . . .'

Willow grinned. 'It's OK,' she said. 'I know about Hoozles.'

Ben was so relieved, he flopped back against the side of the boat. Spike flapped his tail and said, 'Hello, matey,' to Toby. Willow giggled when Toby put out his hand and tried to shake Spike's fin.

'Hoozles are just the best toys ever, aren't they?' said Ben.

Willow looked fondly at Toby. 'Absolutely the best. Well, almost all of them.' She told Ben about Croc, the naughty orange crocodile

Hoozle, who once tried to steal
Toby's pocket heart.

Ben frowned. 'He'd better not try
to steal Spike's. Look.' He showed

Willow the baby
shark's tooth in
Spike's pocket. Like
all pocket hearts,
it was a symbol of
the special bond
owners shared with
their Hoozles. 'I really love Spike,' he
said. 'I've had him for two years.'

'I've had Toby much longer than

that,' said Willow. 'Ever since I was a baby.'

'How long have you known the Hoozle secret?' asked Ben.

'Ever since we came to stay with Auntie Suzy for the summer.'

'I've known about it longer than that,' said Ben. 'I found out Spike was alive the day after I got him, when I dropped him overboard into the sea. He swam back to me. I was so surprised I nearly fell overboard myself!'

Willow laughed.

Then Ben said, 'We're even. You've had Toby the longest, and I've known the Hoozle secret the longest!'

Toby and Spike had gone off together and settled in the centre of a red and white lifebelt. They lay on their backs giggling at the antics of the greedy gulls that swooped above the boat, hoping for someone to throw them a titbit.

Ben showed Willow different sorts of sea birds. Soon they were close enough to Summertown Cove to see puffins sitting on a grassy ledge halfway up the cliff. Ben pointed out one bobbing on the water nearby.

'It's funny-looking, with that big orange beak,' Willow said, 'I– '

There was a loud juddering sound. *Sharkfin*'s engine coughed twice, then stopped.

'What's happened?' cried a young woman with long hair.

Everyone spoke at once.

'We've broken down.'

'But why?'

'I know what it is!' the long-haired woman said in a trembly voice.

Willow gulped. She knew what the woman was going to say.

'It's the ghost of Six-Fingered Jim!'

Chapter Three

'Nothing to worry about,' said
Captain Price. 'Little problem with
the engine. Soon have it fixed. Ben!'
he called. 'I need a hand.'

Ben was already on his way.

'I hope the captain can mend the
boat,' said Toby. 'Otherwise we might

have to stay here for ever, and there's
nothing for you and Freddie and
Suzy to eat.'

Willow laughed.
'Even if he
couldn't mend
it, someone
would come
and help.'

She'd barely finished speaking
when, with a cough, a hiccup and a
splutter, the engine started.

The passengers cheered.

Captain Price appeared, shaking

his head and wiping his hands on an oily rag. There was a long shiny brown ribbon of seaweed draped over his arm. 'Most strange,' he said to Auntie Suzy. 'This seaweed was caught in the engine. Now how could it possibly get in there? I've had it caught round the propeller before, but never inside the engine.' He shrugged and flung the seaweed overboard. Then he took the wheel. 'Right, me hearties, next stop Summertown Cove and the amazing caves!'

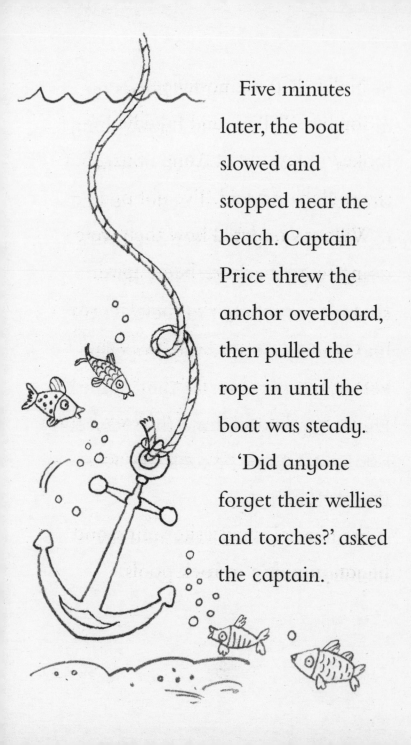

Five minutes later, the boat slowed and stopped near the beach. Captain Price threw the anchor overboard, then pulled the rope in until the boat was steady.

'Did anyone forget their wellies and torches?' asked the captain.

'No!' yelled the passengers.

Torches! Willow and Freddie looked anxiously at Auntie Suzy, but she smiled and said, 'I've got one.'

Willow wondered how they were going to get to shore, but Captain Price showed them that *Sharkfin* was moored against a shelf of rock that was just below the surface of the water. He slid the gangplank over the side. 'Walk down that and wade to the beach,' he said.

Freddie splashed ashore first and began jumping in rock pools.

Ben and Willow went together and
waited by the cave entrance as
everyone gathered round.

Willow cuddled Toby tightly as she
peered inside. She could just imagine
Six-Fingered Jim dragging his
treasure chest into the gloomy caves.

'I wish I could find the treasure,' she told Ben, 'but, suppose I did, and then I disappeared because of the curse and was never, ever seen again?'

Ben looked at her for a few moments before speaking. 'I think I know where the treasure's h

Willow's heart leapt, but then she thought, *He's making it up. He couldn't possibly know.* 'Prove it,' she said.

'Okay,' said Ben. 'I will.' He tapped Captain Price on the shoulder. 'Uncle, can I take Willow to see my favourite part of the caves, instead of coming on the tour?'

The captain looked at Auntie Suzy.

'If it's safe, Ben,' said Auntie Suzy.

'I've been there loads of times,' he said.

The captain looked at his watch. 'You have an hour. Only go to

the caves you've explored before, and meet us right here. Got your torch?'

'Yes,' said Ben.

'Remember,' said Auntie Suzy. 'One hour.'

'I've got my watch,' said Willow, holding out her wrist. 'It has a little light in it, so I can tell the time in the dark.' She pressed a button. 'See?'

'Off you go, then,' said Auntie Suzy, 'and look after those Hoozles.'

'We will!'

Ben led the way, shining his torch on the damp rock.

Willow was excited, but she also felt a little bit scared. Suppose they got lost? Suppose the torch battery ran out? Suppose . . . She suddenly realised Toby was poking her with his paw.

'Willow, you're squeezing me too hard,' he said.

'Sorry, Toby,' she said, giving him

a quick kiss. 'I'm a bit nervous. But don't tell Ben that,' she added quickly. 'If he's brave enough to wander off through dark caves and passages, then so am I!'

Chapter Four

'Wow!' Willow completely forgot
her nerves as Ben led her into a vast
cavern. He flashed the torch around
slowly. Pointed rocks stood like
upside-down ice cream cones. Some
were tiny, and some were three times
her height.

'Stalagmites!' said Willow.

'And stalactites,' said Ben, shining the light upwards. Hanging from the roof was a forest of rocks, glistening wetly, like icicles. 'Watch where you step,' he went on. 'There

are little pools all over the place, and some of them are deep.'

'Can I walk?' Toby asked.

Willow put him down. 'Stay near the torch light.'

'This way,' Ben called.

Willow followed the pool of torch light through a twisting rock passage and came out into an even bigger cavern. There was a wide, flat open space in the middle with a rock like a long bench. She stood on it to look around. The light from the torch bounced back from rock pools and

wet walls, making it easy to see all
around.

'Hey!' Ben shouted suddenly,
making Willow jump. His voice went,
'Hey … ey … ey … ey … ey … ey!'

Toby tried to scramble up beside
Willow. She lifted him on to the flat
rock, and he clutched her leg.

'It's okay,' she said.
'It's just an echo.
Listen.' And she
cupped her mouth
with her hands and
yelled. 'Tobeee!'

'... bee ... bee ... bee ... bee,' went the echo.

Toby stared around in wonder. Then he cried out, 'Spike, can you hear me?' and the echo came back, '... me ... me ... me ... me ... me!'

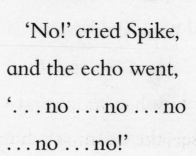

'No!' cried Spike, and the echo went, '... no ... no ... no ... no ... no!'

Toby giggled and shouted back. The two Hoozles had a wonderful time making echoes, until Willow called out, 'Stop!'

Back came the echo. '. . . op . . . op . . . op . . . op . . . op!' and everybody laughed.

Willow noticed a faint glow. She got Ben to shine the torch towards it. There was a wide tunnel with daylight at the end.

Ben explained that it was another entrance into the caves. 'Can you see, the opening's shaped a bit like a tiger's mouth? That's why I reckon the treasure's near here.'

Willow had to agree about the cave entrance looking like a tiger's mouth. She could make out rocks shaped like great sharp teeth. But she wasn't convinced that Ben was right about the treasure. 'If it *was* here, surely you would have found it already,' she said, jumping down from the flat rock.

'I've only explored half this cavern,' said Ben. 'The treasure could be hidden in one of the little passages,

or under a heap of rocks, or – or
anywhere. Look over here.' He made
his way towards the cavern wall,
dodging puddles. Suddenly,
he yelped and fell.
Willow watched
in horror as the
torch bounced
away from
Ben straight
towards a
rock pool.
Splash!

Everything went dark.

A small, shaky voice said, 'Willow? Who put the light out?'

'It's all right, Toby,' she said, switching on the light in her watch. She could just make out Ben, crouching on the ground. 'Are you okay?' she called to him.

'Yes,' he called back.

'Is Spike all right?' Willow asked, going to see.

'I'm squashed,' grumbled Spike. 'Ben landed right on top of me when he fell.'

'Sorry, Spike,' said Ben, brushing dirt off his Hoozle. 'But, Willow, that wasn't an accident. Look!' He pulled her arm towards him, so her watch light shone downwards.

Willow peered into the glow. She could just make out something like a thick thread. 'What is it?'

'Fishing line,' said Ben, and
he showed her where it was tied
between two rocks.

Willow gasped. 'Someone put that
there on purpose, to stop anyone
going any further? Maybe . . . maybe
it was Six-Fingered Jim?' she said in a
shaky voice.

'No chance,' said Ben. 'I've been
this way before, remember, and
I've never seen this.' He frowned.
'Whoever it is, they're not stopping
me. Let's get that torch back.'

Willow sat Toby on a small round

 rock while she
and Ben pushed
their sleeves
up and fished
around in the
rock pool.

'We'll never
reach it,' said Ben. 'The water's too
deep.'

'Then you need a good swimmer,'
said Spike. 'Don't you worry. I'll
get it for you.' He used his fins to
wiggle to the pool, then slipped in
and disappeared from sight. A few

moments later, the torch appeared on
top of the water, balanced on Spike's
head. Willow grabbed it.

Ben lifted Spike out. 'You're a star!'
he said.

'You really are,' said Willow. She shook the torch. 'Will it work?' she wondered.

'It should do,' said Ben. 'It's waterproof.'

Willow switched it on. It was fine. 'There, Toby,' she said. 'That's better, isn't it?'

There was no reply.

'Toby?' Willow turned. '*Toby*!' In a panic, she flashed the torch all round the cave.

Toby was gone.

Chapter Five

'...bee...eee...eee...ee...ee,'
went the echo, as Willow shouted
desperately for her bear.

'Toby, where are you?' cried Ben.

'...yooo...ooo...ooo...oo...
oo,' went the echo.

Suddenly, Willow froze. Had

she heard something? 'Shh,' she whispered. 'Listen!'

Ben stood still.

The sudden silence was broken by muffled grunts and growls.

'It's Toby!' Willow cried. 'He's hurt, or stuck somewhere. Follow the sounds.'

But no matter how hard they tried, they couldn't make out where the noises were coming from. Every footstep echoed, and even Toby's muffled cries created their own faint echoes.

Ben's torch lit up dark corners and cracks in the rock, but there was no sign of the little blue Hoozle.

Willow peered around, her eyes following the torch light. *Oh, Toby,* she thought. *Where are you?*

Suddenly, she froze. On the round rock, where she'd last seen her

Hoozle, something gleamed. Willow
snatched the torch from Ben and
shone it on the rock. Yes, there was
something there! It was gold, and it
looked like ... 'A
coin!'
She darted
forward and
snatched it up.
'Look, Ben,'
she gasped.
'Pirate gold!'
Suddenly, a terrible shiver of fear
ran through her body. 'Oh no,'

she groaned. 'It's the curse. Anyone who looks for Six-Fingered Jim's treasure disappears. We came to look for it and now Toby has vanished!'

Willow stared at the gold coin clutched in her hand. It was bent. She was sure it had been completely flat before. 'What's going on?' she wondered, as she examined it more closely.

Ben picked at the coin's edges. 'It's not made of gold,' he said. 'This is a chocolate coin.' He looked thoughtful. 'Someone's trying to cause trouble here, Willow. First the seaweed in the engine, then the line that tripped me up, and now . . . this.'

Willow's eyes widened. 'You're right. And I know exactly who it is.' She turned and shouted into the darkness. 'Croc? *Croc*! I know it's you! Where are you?'

The only reply was an echoing laugh from the mean orange crocodile Hoozle. The sound bounced off the cave walls. It was impossible to tell where it came from.

Willow spun round and shouted

again. 'Your seaweed trick didn't work, did it? You're not so clever!'

'Oh yes, I am,' called Croc. 'You'll never find out where your precious Toby is hidden. You can't even find me because of all the echoes.'

Willow knew he was right.

Ben pulled at her arm. 'We'll have to go soon. Our hour's nearly up. If we're not back on time, my uncle and Suzy will be really worried.'

Willow stared at him, shocked. She couldn't believe what he was saying. 'No!' she cried. 'We can't leave without Toby!'

Chapter Six

'We must do something,' Willow said.

'And we have to do it quickly,' said Ben.

Willow thought hard. *Croc can't resist a chance to upset Hoozles and their owners.*

She whispered in Ben's ear, 'Croc

will come out of hiding if he thinks
he can steal Spike's pocket heart.'

'No crocodile could get the better
of my Hoozle.'

'Dead right,' said Spike.

Willow cleared her throat loudly
and said, 'Ben, let's look for Toby
behind that big rock, right over there
by the cave wall. Spike, stay here
by yourself and keep an eye out for
Toby. You'll be quite safe.'

'I know I will,' said Spike.

Ben balanced the torch on a rock
so that it lit up most of the cavern.

He and Willow made their way to
the wall, climbing carefully over
small rocks and dodging pools.
They slipped behind the big rock
and peeped out to see what was
happening.

A few moments later, Croc appeared from a small opening beside the tunnel that led to the tiger's mouth. He scuttled across to where Spike lay. Willow was about to rush to Spike's rescue, but Ben held her back. 'Watch,' he said.

As Croc reached out to grab the puffer fish Hoozle, Spike puffed himself up into a big ball shape – with scary-looking spikes!

'Scram!' he said.

Croc was so shocked that he fell backwards into a rock pool. *Splash*!

'Wow!' said Willow.

Ben grinned. 'That's what puffer fish do,' he said proudly. 'Come on, don't stand there staring. Let's go and catch Croc!'

But as they made their way
carefully back to Spike, Croc
scrambled out of the pool
and scurried away into the
darkness. He was soaking
wet, and kept slipping on
the slimy rock floor.
His grumbles echoed
round the cave
and faded away
as Croc fled.

'Now don't bother us anymore!' Spike called, shrinking back to his normal size.

'That was amazing,' Willow told him. 'You looked really fearsome.'

'That's the idea,' said Spike. 'What do we do now?'

'Find Toby, of course.'

'And quickly,' said Ben, 'or we'll be late.'

Willow took the torch and headed for Croc's hiding place, near the tunnel leading to the tiger's mouth. She peered between two great

stalagmites, and there, at last, was her
little blue bear. He'd
been tied up and
gagged with long
ribbons of tough,
shiny brown seaweed.
'Toby!' she cried,
pulling the
horrible
stuff away
from his
mouth.
'Are you
all right?'

Toby sat up and spat. 'Pthyerr! That stuff's disgusting,' he said.

Willow sat on a flat rock to untie him. Once he was free, she hugged him so hard he began to wriggle. She leant on one of the stalagmites as she stood up, and noticed a pattern of rough bumps in the rock. One, two, three, four, five, six. Six bumps. Six-Fingered Jim! Suddenly, the stalagmite wobbled. She snatched Toby up and jumped away from it.

'Look!' cried Ben. 'Behind you!'

She spun round. With a heavy

scraping noise, a section of rock slid
to one side. Behind was . . .

'A secret cave!' Willow said. 'Oh,
Ben, let's look inside.'

'Not another cave,' Toby groaned.
'I want to be outside in the sunshine.'

Willow gave him a big hug to
keep warm. 'We won't be long,' she
said, shining the torch into the secret
cave. In the middle of the floor was
a large, ancient, wooden chest. '*Ben!*'
she gasped.

He followed her inside. His eyes
widened when he saw the chest.

Together they lifted the lid, then they
looked at each other, eyes shining!

'Pirate clothes!' said Ben, taking
out a big hat with an ostrich feather
in it.

Willow pulled out a short, curved sword. 'A cutlass!'

'Maps!' said Ben. 'And a telescope.'

Willow found a pair of leather gloves, and tried them on. They reached halfway up her arms. 'Look at me in pirate gloves, Ben.'

She felt Toby poking her arm. 'What's the matter?'

With a shaky paw, he pointed to her right hand. She looked at it and gasped. The glove had an extra finger!

'Wow!' said Willow. 'That proves it. This *must* be the treasure of Six-Fingered Jim.' Then her stomach did a flip-flop. 'Oh no! The curse! Anyone who looks for the treasure is cursed.'

Ben's mouth opened and closed before he spoke. 'And we *found* it. Oh, Willow, we're all cursed!'

Spike spoke up. 'Stop being so daft,' he said. 'Willow and Toby haven't disappeared, and nor have you, Ben. I don't think I can have disappeared, since you're all staring at me, so

I reckon the curse is a load of old rubbish.'

There was a moment of silence, then they all giggled. With laughter echoing through the caverns, they  hurried back to meet the others.

'Just think,' said Willow, 'if Croc hadn't got up to his tricks, we'd never have found the treasure.' She thought for a moment. 'Ben, let's keep this to ourselves. Don't let's tell the grown-ups.'

'Okay,' said Ben. 'It'll be our secret. No one's to say a word. Right, Toby and Spike?'

'Hoozle's honour,' they said together.

When they arrived back at the little beach, the last passenger was just climbing aboard. Captain Price tapped his wrist, as if to say, 'You're late,' but he was smiling. Mr Squawk wiggled his wing tip, just a little, so the captain couldn't see.

'Did you have a good time?' asked
Auntie Suzy.

'Brilliant,' said Willow and Ben
together.

Then Ben asked Auntie Suzy, 'Can
Willow come on the boat with me
again?'

She smiled. 'Of course.'

'Great!' said Willow. 'We could have a picnic in Summertown Cove with our Hoozles, and play pirates.'

As they climbed aboard *Sharkfin,* Willow turned to Ben and grinned. What fun they could have with the treasure of Six-Fingered Jim!

Very slowly, so no one else would notice, Mr Squawk winked.

Willow giggled and winked back. 'Perhaps we could invite one other Hoozle,' she said.

'Weigh anchor!' cried out Captain

Price. 'All aboard for Summertown!'

'And set a course for our next Hoozle adventure!' Willow whispered to Toby. She gave him a big cuddle as *Sharkfin* pulled out of the cove and set sail for home.

Get ready for even more

Magic Toyshop adventures!

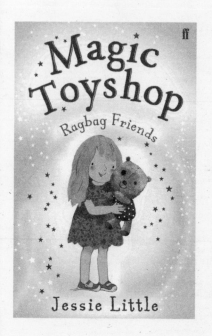